My First

# You Can, Too!

by Wiley Blevins
Illustrated by Ken Bowser

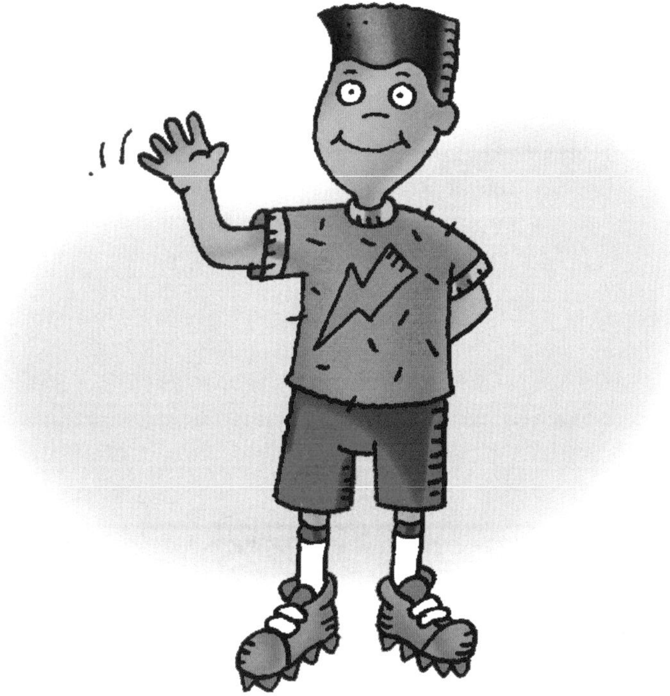

Dan.

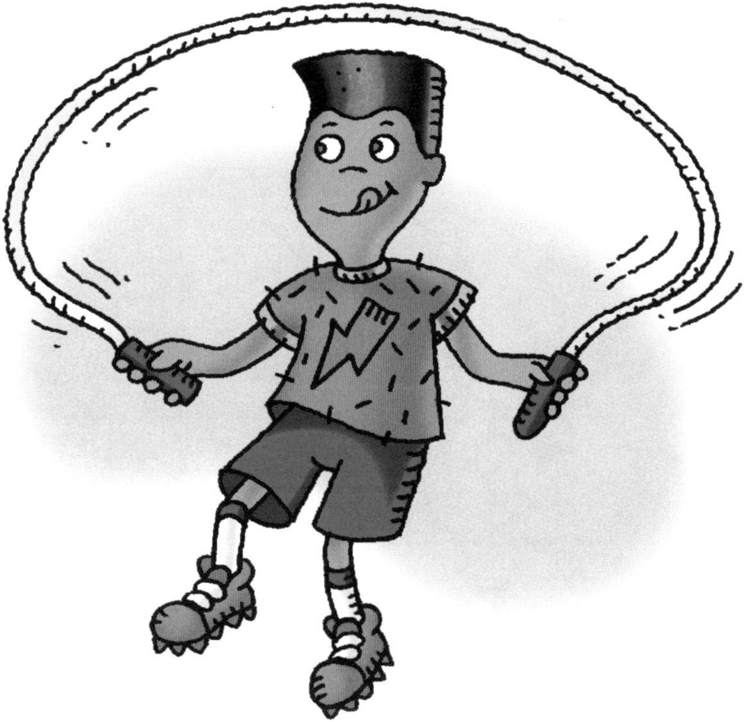

Dan can 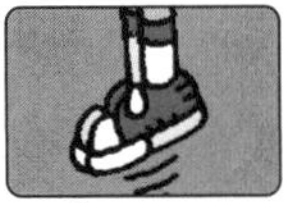 .

jump

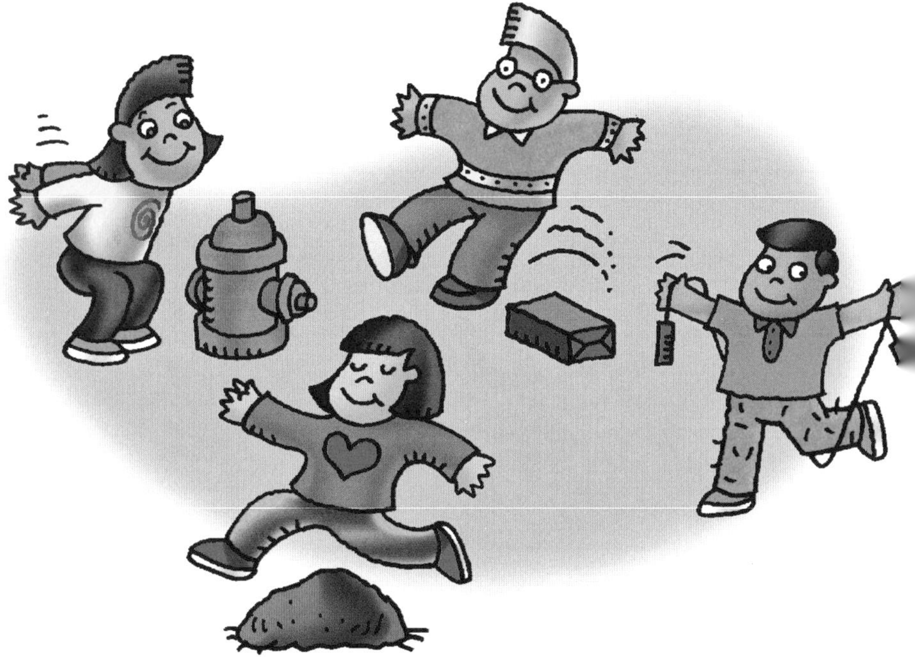

Can you?

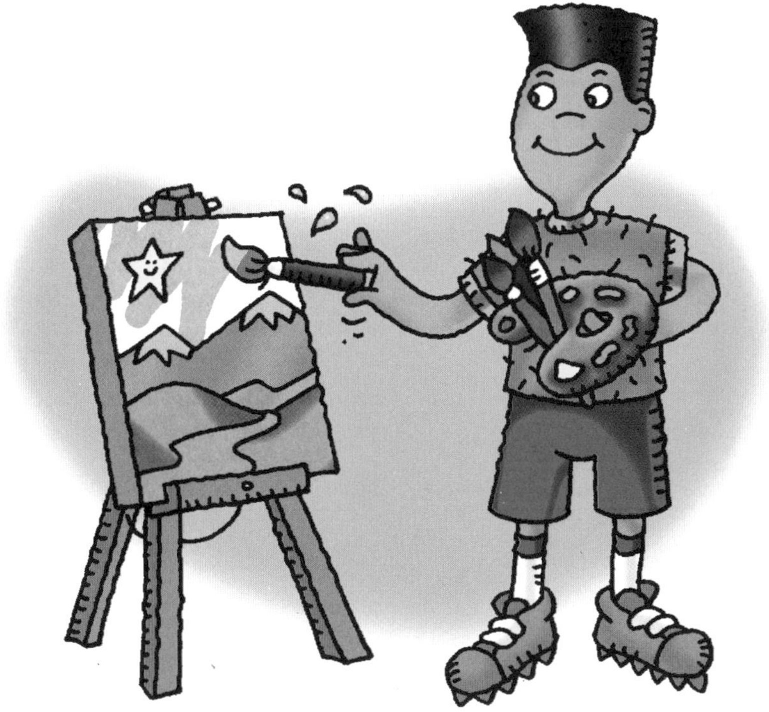

Dan can 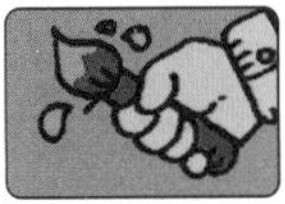.

paint

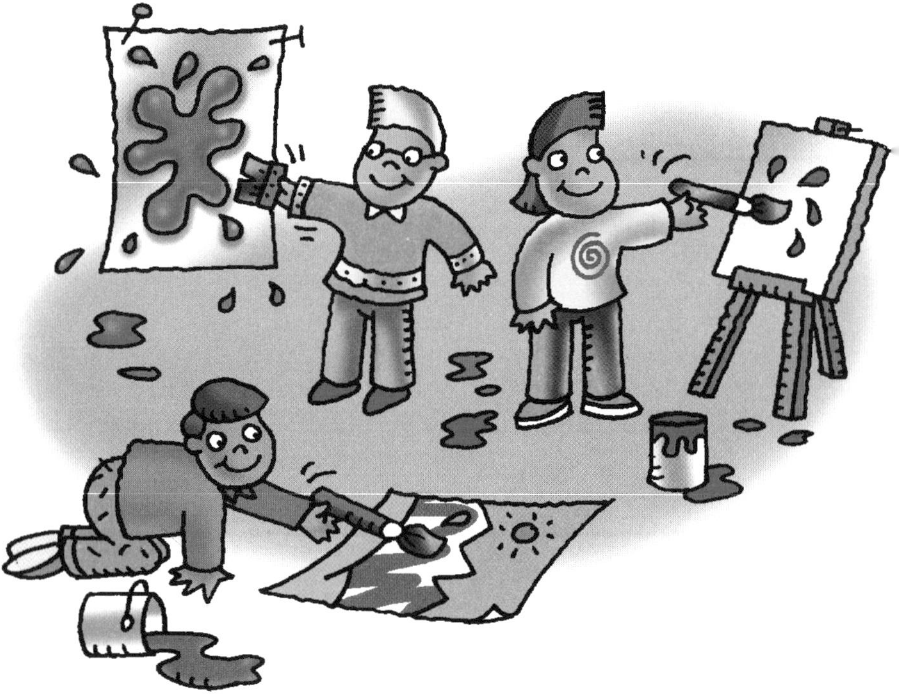

Can you?

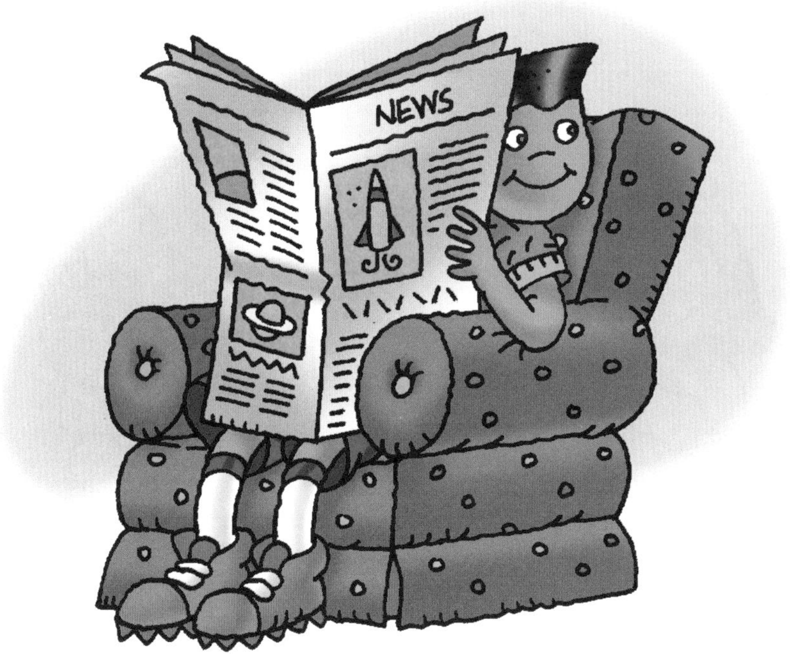


Dan can 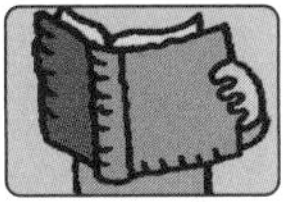 .

read

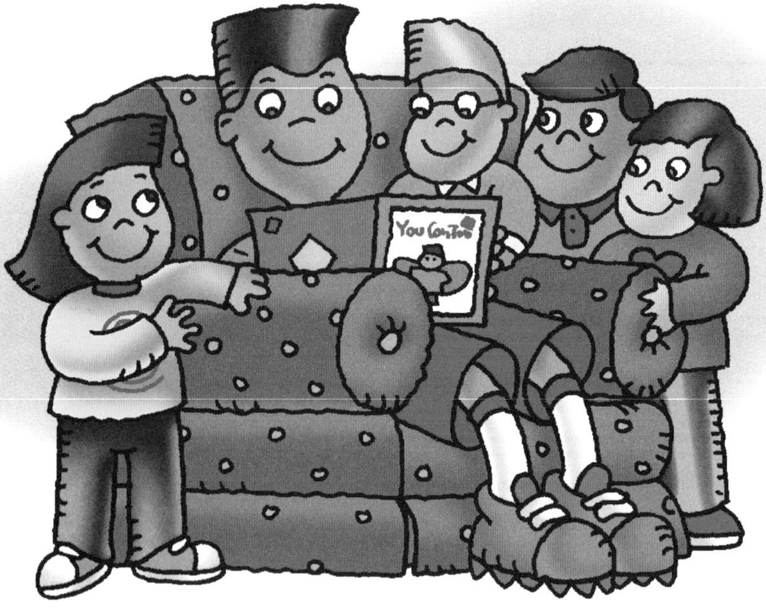


You can, too!